BOOK #6

OTTO UNDERCOVER

★BRAIN FREEZE★

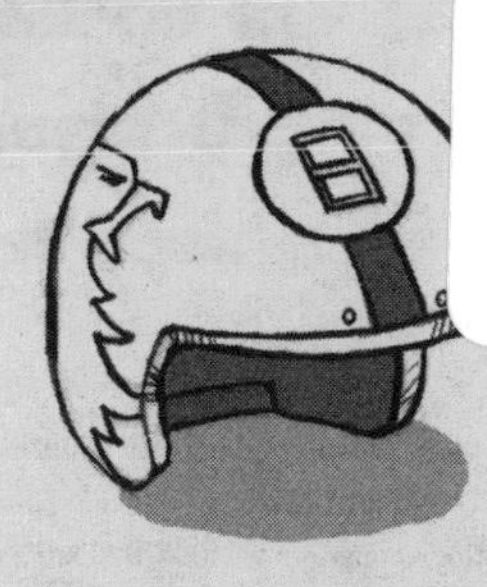

RHEA PERLMAN

ILLUSTRATED BY

DAN SANTAT

KATHERINE TEGEN BOOKS

An Imprint of HarperCollins*Publishers*

This book is dedicated to
everyone who loves Raisinets.

Otto Undercover #6: Brain Freeze

For information address HarperCollins Children's Books, a division of HarperCollins Publishers, 1350 Avenue of the Americas, New York, NY 10019.
www.harpercollinschildrens.com

Library of Congress Cataloging-in-Publication Data is available.
ISBN 978-0-06-075505-8 (pbk. bdg.)

Typography by Jennifer Heuer
1 2 3 4 5 6 7 8 9 10
❖
First Edition

CONTENTS

USEFUL INFORMATION

eye
Eee YiiiY Eee

SECRET FILES

JAKE EBOY

Alias: Otto Pillip
Occupations:
- Secret Agent
- Racecar Driver
- Inventor
- Singer/Songwriter

Problem Area: Can Only Sing the Note E
Legal Guardians: The Aunts
Hobby: Words...Especially Palindromes, Anagrams, and Backward Words

ELEANOR AND HOGARTH EBOY

Occupations:
- Senior Secret Agents

Immediate Family:
- Son, Jake Eboy

Whereabouts: On the Lam

AUNT FOOFOO AKA AUNT OOFOOF

Alias: Uncle FroFro AKA Uncle OrfOrf
Occupations:
- Assistant Secret Agent
- Pit Crew Co-Chief

Hobby: World-Famous Chef

AUNT FIFI AKA AUNT IFIF

Alias: Uncle FriFri AKA Uncle IrfIrf
ccupations:
Assistant Secret Agent
Pit Crew Co-Chief
bbies: Tap Dancing/Singing
oblem Area: Can Only Sing the Note A-flat

RACECAR
Designer: Otto Pillip
Driver: Otto Pillip
Feature: Fastest Car on Earth
Special Features:
· Claw
· Vacu-Zap
· Voice Command
· A Million More Things
Extra-Special Feature: Can Morph into Other Vehicles
A
B
C
D
E
F
GADGETS
A. Pocket Watch Remote Control B. Multi-Functional Radar Tracking and Guiding Ring with Infrared Flashlight C. Solar/Lunar Power Helmet D. Computer Shoe E. Freckle/Pimple 2-Way Global Positioning Transmitters F. Kangaroo Jumping Shoes

Two Things You Should Know Besides How to Fart and Blame It on the Dog, and How to Belch the Alphabet

1. **Palindromes**

are words that are spelled exactly the same way backward and forward.

EXAMPLES:

Otto, **Racecar**, and **pooch coop**

2. **Anagrams**

are words that become other words when their letters are all scrambled up.

EXAMPLES:

the eyes is an anagram for **they see**

decimal point is an anagram for **I'm a dot in place**

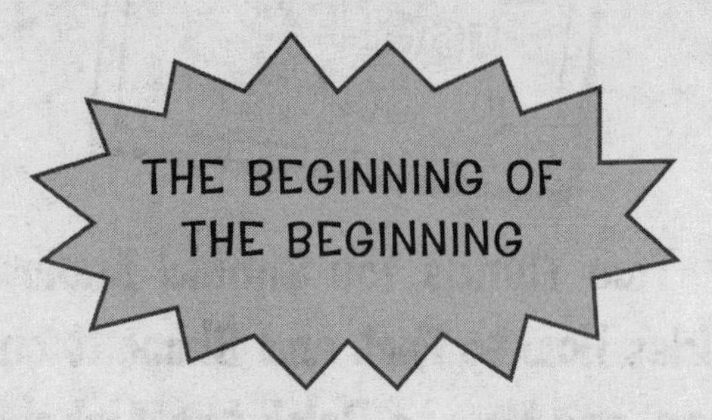

October 31

It was Halloween and Otto had three things on his mind: trick-or-treating, rock and roll, and Raisinets.

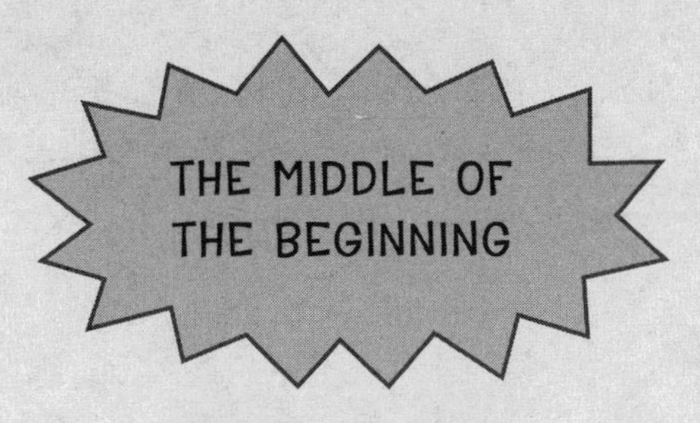

The Treat

Otto was obsessed with Raisinets. They had raisins, they had chocolate, and they didn't have any lousy nuts to ruin them. They were the most perfect candy in the world.

The Plan

Tonight he was trick-or-treating with his best friend, the tiny toddler ***L'il Mellem***. ***L'il Mellem*** was going as ***L'il Otto***. ***Mellem*** wanted them to look like twins, so Otto was going as himself.

Racecar had a costume too. Otto had secretly been working on it for months. It was a surprise disguise. All he needed was to get back to the garage for a couple of finishing touches and it would be ready.

After trick-or-treating, Otto and ***Mellem*** were meeting up with ***Mellem***'s ***dad***, ***Donod***, and their band, the Screaming Oranges, for a **gig** at the Halloween concert

*L'il Mellem, L'il Otto, Donod, dad, and **gig** are palindromes.*

at Town Tower. When it was over, ***Mellem*** and ***Donod*** were coming back to The Aunts' house for a sleepover.

That's where the Raisinets came in. Otto and ***Mellem*** were going to trade in all their lame trick-or-treat loot for the little chocolate-covered raisins and eat them until their stomachs burst.

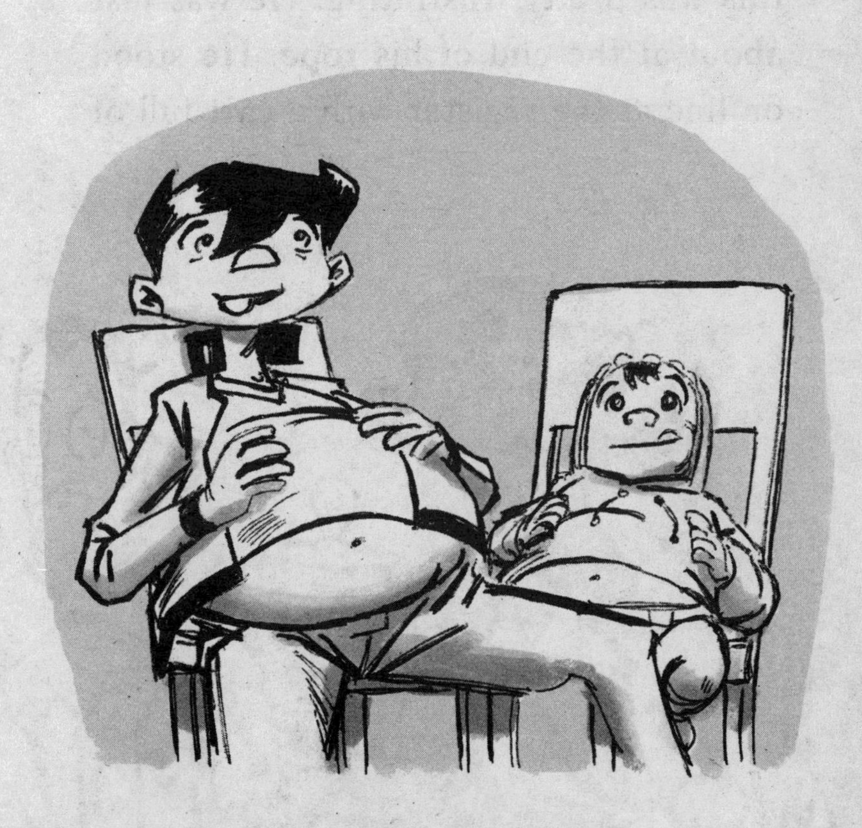

October 31–4:45 P.M.

Otto and Aunt FooFoo had visited 15 stores, and they were all out of Raisinets. Otto was a patient guy, but this was pretty frustrating. He was just about at the end of his rope. He stood on line at the register with a cart full of

roasted quail eggs and frozen veal shanks, because his aunt could never go to a store and just get what they came for. Now FooFoo was running around aisle two looking for ***Feeble Tom's Motel Beef*** and ***Pint a' Catnip***. It was getting dark. Some kids roamed around the store in their costumes. The kid in front of Otto was painted green and said he was ***Neil, an alien***. A weird guy dressed as a chicken stood behind Otto in line.

Feeble Tom's Motel Beef, Pint a' Catnip, *and* ***Neil, an alien*** *are palindromes.*

Cha-ching slam is onomatopoeia.

He had dandruff all over his feathers.

"Hurry, Aunt OofOof," yelled Otto. "It's almost our turn."

"I'm coming, Ottie," she yelled back.

Cha-ching slam. Otto heard the sounds of the register in his head as words, which made him nervous. This phenomenon was called onomatopoeia, and it only happened to him when things were going really good or really bad, and really good was out of the question this time.

Footnote in the Middle of the Page aka Belly-Button Note

Onomatopoeia are words that sound like their meanings. Onomatopoeia may be contagious. The only known cure is sticking cotton in your ears. Onomatopoeia backwards is aieopotamono.

FooFoo came bounding across the

store with a pile of food in her arms. ***Crash! Ba-boom bong.*** She bumped into Otto, dropping all her stuff on the floor.

"Next person," said the cashier, looking to the chicken-guy behind Otto.

"No please, wait a minute," said Otto. As he bent down to pick up FooFoo's

Crash! Ba-boom bong *is onomatopoeia.*

things, his remote control pocket watch accidentally fell to the ground. Otto almost had a heart attack. The flakey guy bent down to help him pick up the watch. Otto snatched it away before the guy could get a good look at all the secret compartments.

Otto would have been better off if he had gotten a good look at the flakey guy.

It was his old enemy, the car thief Paulie Prat.

12 Hours Earlier–October 31–4:45 A.M.

Ralphie and Paulie had been locked up in a makeshift jail on the Yazoo Racetrack since Otto caught them stealing Racecar during the first book of this series, which is called *Otto Undercover—Born to Drive*, in case you haven't read it, which you should because it's the best book ever written, so right after you finish this book drop everything and go get it.

Ralphie was still trying to dig his way out of the geyser that had sprung up when he crashed through the ground, and Paulie was still trying to fish him out.

At 4:45 A.M., for the first time since he cast his fishing line into the gushing geyser, Paulie got a bite. It was a big one.

"Eeeyeooooouuuuw!" bubbled up a scream from deep underground.

"Hang on, big guy, I'm bringin' you up," yelled Paulie.

The hook was lodged in Ralphie's butt.

Paulie, who was incredibly strong, jerked hard on the line.

Ralphie flew up and over the walls of the outdoor jail. The force brought Paulie along with him.

Paulie looked around.

"We're free," he said.

"My butt hurts," said Ralphie.

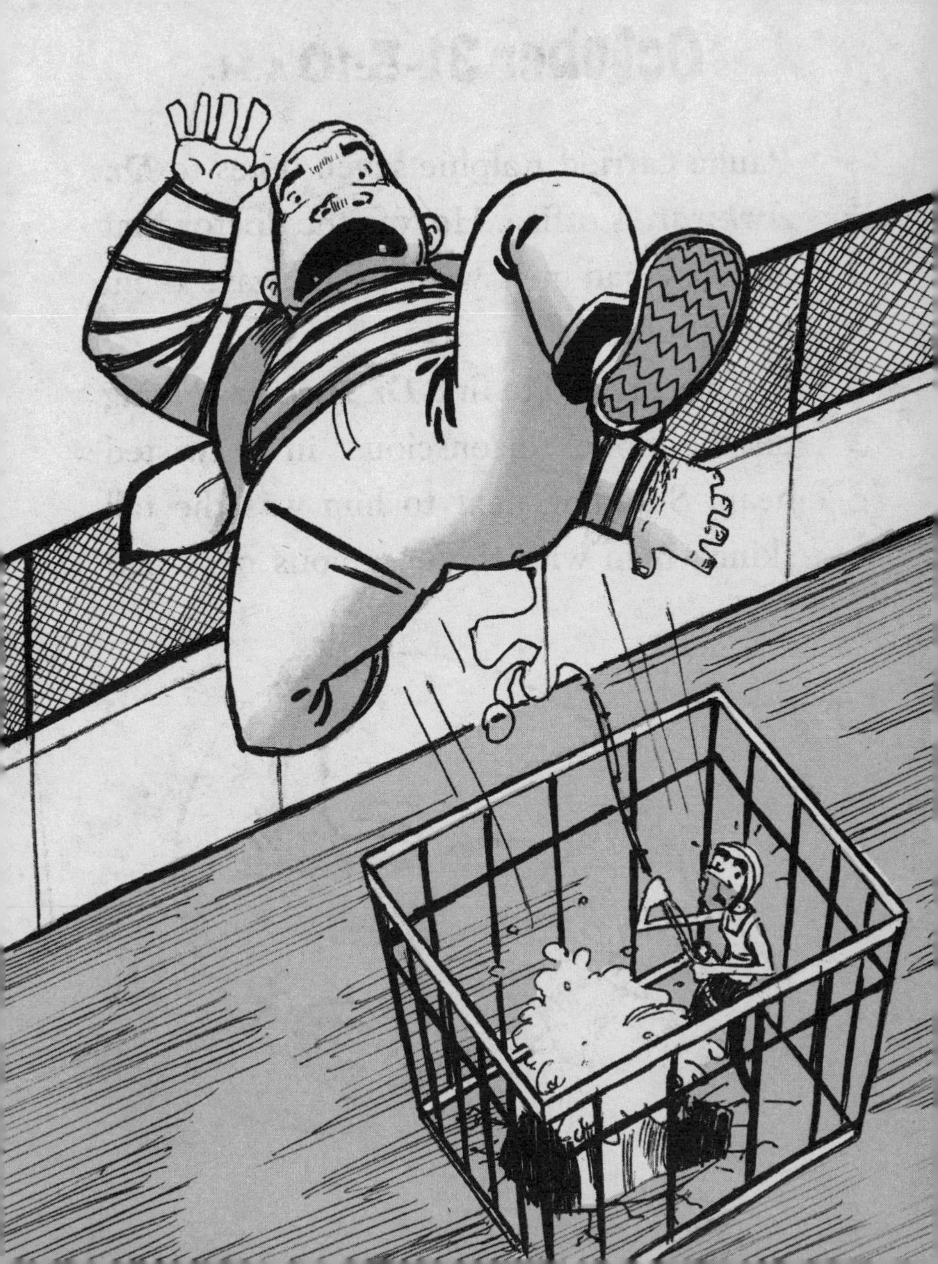

October 31-5:10 A.M.

Dr. Awkward is a palindrome.

Paulie carried Ralphie seven miles to ***Dr. Awkward***'s office. He was the doctor that all lousy bad guys went to. He gave them a discount.

They arrived to find ***Dr. Awkward*** lying on the floor, unconscious, in a twisted heap. Standing next to him was the tall skinny man with the enormous neck and

the long dangling head . . .

the archenemy of Otto's parents.

October 31-5:10 A.M. plus 30 seconds

Paulie immediately recognized the legendary outlaw I. Skreem. He dropped Ralphie on the floor and bowed deeply.

"I am honored to be in the same doctor's office with the lousiest bad guy in the history of the world since the beginning of time before there were shoes or pizza, a hundred years ago," said Paulie humbly, and dumbly.

"My butt hurts," said Ralphie miserably.

"Hold up my heeeaaaad," whined I. Skreem. "Do you want to be in my gaaaannnng?"

"Yes, sire," said Paulie.

"Then hold up my heeeaaaad," said I. Skreem.

Paulie picked up I. Skreem's head.

"Let's get out of heeerrrre," whined I. Skreem.

"Can the doctor take this hook out of my butt first?" asked Ralphie.

"Nooooo," said I. Skreem, "he's out of order. He reinstalled my vocal chords, but he didn't fix my neeeeck. So I screamed at him reeeallly haaaard."

"But my butt hurts," said Ralphie.

"Stop whiiiiiiining," whined I. Skreem. "I'll take out your stupid hooook." He pulled the hook out of Ralphie's butt. Ralphie screamed.

"That's the puniest scream I ever

Butt tub is a palindrome.

heeeeard," said I. Skreem.

"Sit in this ***butt tub***. It's full of alco-hooool." He pushed Ralphie into the tub, which made him scream again.

"That was even punieeeer," said I. Skreem. "From now on, I'll do all the screaming in my gaaaannng. It's called the Ice Cream Gang. Let's gooooooo!"

Back to Otto

Otto and FooFoo left the market and pulled out of the lot in Racecar. They hadn't gone two blocks when Otto noticed a backward stop sign. It said ***Pots***. His ***eye*** started twitching.

***Pots** is backward for **stop**.*
***Eye** is a palindrome.*

"Oh no," he said. "I hope we're not going to have to go on a mission on Halloween." ***Hissss!*** A bus turned in front of them. A poster on the side showed an advertisement for a soap detergent called ***Armpit Not Blue Lint***.

"I can't wait to try that new soap powder," said FooFoo. "A giant box of it fell right into my shopping cart at the market."

"Let me have it, please," said Otto.

"All right," said FooFoo, handing it to

Hissss *is onomatopoeia.*
Armpit Not Blue Lint *is an anagram for* ***Important Bulletin.***

him, "but it'll work better with water."

Otto rifled through the box of soap. Inside, he found a pamphlet.

We interrupt our regularly scheduled book to bring you a

pamphlet.

The Tall Skinny Man with the Enormous Neck and the Long Dangling Head

A Scary Story

By Anonymous

Warning!!!!

Some episodes in this pamphlet contain violence. Please have a jacket handy to put over your eyes.

Once upon a time there was a little boy whose head was right on top of his neck, like everyone else's. His name was Igor Skreemwich.

One day, Igor's ball rolled down into a sewer. Angry because his arm wasn't long enough to reach the ball, he screamed.

"Eeeeeeyiiiiiiyeeeeee!"

His scream was so loud that the ground shook and the sidewalk cracked.

A man who happened to be walking by was hit by the scream.

The sound went straight to his brain, and gave him a supersonic ice-cream headache. He twisted to the left, he

101 and Eeeeeeyiiiiiiyeeeeee are palindromes.

twisted to the right, he did a few dance steps and fell to the ground unconscious.

Igor noticed that the man was wearing a big sparkling diamond ring. He pried it off greedily and put it on his own finger.

"Preeetty," whined Igor.

The next day when the man woke up,

he could remember nothing. Not even his own name. He had permanent brain freeze. However, he was able to dance extremely well. He went off to join the Russian ballet.

As Igor grew older, he developed some problems. He could not control his temper, he loved shiny jewels, and he was a big whiner.

At first, he tried to use his amazing voice for good. He started ***Eee YiiiY Eee***, the famous secret agent agency. He went after bad guys and captured them with his scream.

But he wasn't getting rich enough. Igor wanted every shiny jewel he saw. Finally, his love for riches got the best of him, and he turned to a life of crime. He left the agency and became a master jewel thief.

333 *and* Eee YiiiY Eee *are palindromes.*

Igor changed his name to I. Skreem.

People were confused. They thought his name was "Ice Cream." But it wasn't. It was I. Skreem.

I. Skreem was a world-class villain. He used his voice to break locks, confuse alarm systems, melt bulletproof glass cases, and deflect laser grids. Nobody could catch him. When I. Skreem screamed, anyone within range would twist to the left, twist to the right, fall to the floor, and sleep all night.

Ten years ago, I. Skreem attempted his most daring robbery ever. He was going to steal the famous crowned jewels from the Tower of London.

He entered the tower and screamed at the two guards. Their brains froze and they collapsed. Then he crept into the jewel room.

He shined his flashlight on the crown inside a bulletproof glass case and screamed again. The glass melted. I. Skreem picked up the crown.

"Preeetty," he whined.

Just then, three figures crept into the tower carrying their brand-new invention, a scream deflector.

They were Eleanor Eboy, Hogarth Eboy, and Adam ***Rabbar***, ***Eee YiiiY Eee***'s best super secret agents.

"Put down the crown and surrender," said Hogarth.

I. Screem screamed.

The scream bounced off the deflector. Hogarth and Eleanor weren't hit. Unfortunately, the edge of the scream nicked Mr. ***Rabbar*** on the butt. He did some dance steps but managed to stay conscious.

The Eboys handcuffed I. Skreem and pinched his lips together with a large paper clip. Without his weapon, I. Skreem was powerless. The Eboys arrested him.

Rabbar is a palindrome.

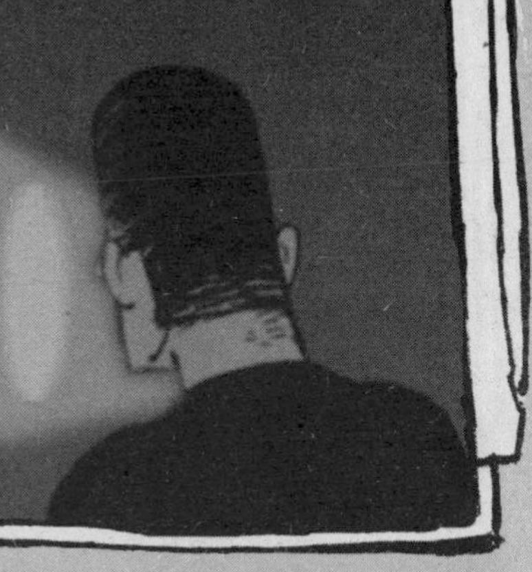

I. Skreem was sent to jail for life. To prevent him from screaming again, a team of prison surgeons removed his toxic vocal chords. But the operation created an unexpected side effect. I. Skreem developed a long narrow head. Twice its normal length, his head dangled from his neck like an overripe butternut squash. Because of gravity, his head and neck continued to grow longer and longer.

I. Skreem swore vengeance on the Eboys.

On his cell wall he wrote:

I'm gonna get those guuuys!!!!

I'M GONNA GET THOSE GUUUYS

Not long after I. Skreem's capture, the Eboys had a child. They quit their secret agent jobs and stayed at home to raise the boy.

They dedicated the rest of their lives to studying I. Skreem's vocal chords. They were developing a synthetic scream that could be used for good, like melting guns and bombs and even enabling people without rhythm to dance.

They kept the chords locked up in a vault in an underground laboratory.

EPISODE 9779

The Eboys were playing with their two-year-old baby son, Jake, when they heard the news that I. Skreem had escaped from prison.

Mom is a palindrome.

With I. Skreem on the loose, the Eboys feared their son was in danger. Going undercover, they vowed to track I. Skreem down. For his own protection they gave Jake a new name and left him with his aunts, FooFoo and FiFi.

"Your new name is Otto Pillip," said Jake's ***mom***.

"What's my new name?" asked FooFoo.

"FooFoo," said the mom.

"I like it!" said FooFoo.

I. Skreem became a legendary outlaw. He stayed with various miserable bad guys over the years, teaching them to dance and giving them jewels that he had stashed away as payment.

Every time the Eboys located him, they wound up fighting the other bad guys while I. Skreem made his getaway.

A few hours ago, I. Skreem's vocal chords disappeared from the vault. The police found his fingerprints and some writing on the wall. It said:

Luckily, I. Skreem still doesn't know where the Eboys are or that they have a child.

Moral of the Story

If you're named Jake and you have parents named Hogarth and Eleanor Eboy . . .

watch out!!!

BACK TO OUR REGULARLY SCHEDULED BOOK

CHAPTER 5

Danger Ahead

Wow is a palindrome.

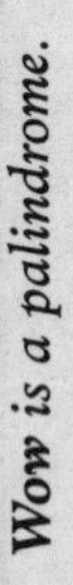

"***Wow***," said Otto, overwhelmed. A million different thoughts rushed through his mind. All of a sudden a really bad one fell into the pit of his stomach.

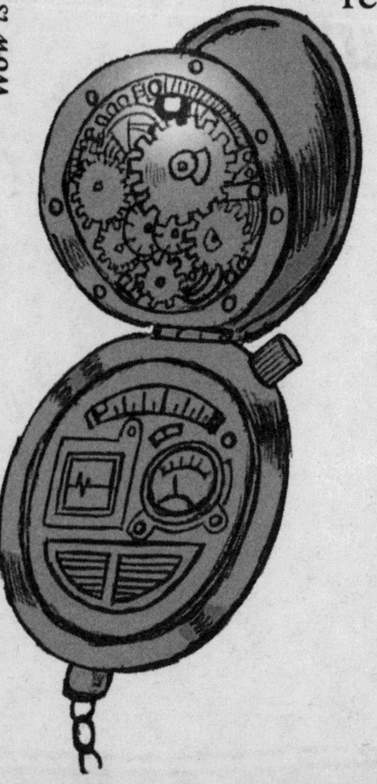

A long time ago his parents had written him a letter. In it they asked Otto to join ***Eee YiiiY Eee***, told him they loved him, and instructed him to destroy the letter. But he didn't. Instead, he converted the words to invisible ink and hid the letter in a secret compartment in his pocket watch. It was the only thing that could connect Otto to his mom and dad.

Otto pulled out his pocket watch and opened the secret compartment.

The letter was gone.

Ba-boom ba-boom. Otto's heart was beating like a bass drum.

Thump-thump *and* ***ba-boom*** *are onomatopoeia.*

Here's What Happened Right after Otto Left the Market

Paulie may have been dressed like a chicken, but he had eagle eyes. He saw the tiny piece of paper that had fallen out of Otto's pocket watch when it dropped on the ground.

"Oooh, paper," said Paulie excitedly.

He picked it up and stuffed it in his beak.

Otto Recovers

"Here's the plan," said Otto. "I'll just do a little quick trick-or-treating with ***Mellem***, and then we'll come back and stay in the house until we get further orders."

"No," said FooFoo.

"What do you mean, no?" asked Otto.

"No trick-or-treating. It's too dangerous. I'm your legal guardian, and I'm putting my foot down."

She did. ***Clump.***

Otto knew that danger lurked everywhere, but he was a kid, and there was no way he was going to miss

Clump *is onomatopoeia.*

out on Halloween.

"You'll have to stay home and eat veal shanks with me and my sister, what's her name?"

Otto knew his aunt FiFi's name, but he hoped he could confuse FooFoo so she'd forget why she'd put her foot down.

"Is it ***Hannah***?" he asked.

"No," said FooFoo.

"***Ava***?"

"No."

"***Klubbulk***?"

"Uhm, possibly."

"***Screwercs***?"

"I don't think so."

"***Frogorf***?"

"Definitely not."

Otto and FooFoo arrived at their house. As they pulled into the garage, they heard a baby wailing.

Hannah, Ava, Klubbulk, Screwercs, and Frogorf are palindromes.

Written in Red

Meanwhile, Paulie returned to Ralphie's mom's house, where the Ice Cream Gang was hiding out.

"It's about time you got back. My arm is killin' me," said Ralphie.

He had been holding I. Skreem's head up for a long time. "What did ya get?" he asked, passing the head to Paulie.

"Uhhh, birdseed," said Paulie.

"We're starving," said Ralphie. "What did ya get birdseed for?"

"I didn't want nobody to know I wasn't really a chicken," said Paulie. "***Sheesh!***"

"What a dumbbell," said Ralphie. "It's a good thing ***Ma has a ham***."

"I got this here piece of paper, too,"

Sheesh *is onomatopoeia.* ***Ma has a ham*** *is a palindrome.*

said Paulie. "I was gonna share it with you, but now I'm not. Here, Mr. Skreem, you can have the whole thing."

"You guys are mooorons," whined I. Skreem. "I'm going to kick you out of my gaaang and scream your eeeyees out of their sockets!"

Ralphie began sweating profusely. Paulie started shaking, his skin flakes flying everywhere.

"Wait a minuuute," said I. Skreem, changing his mind. "This is interestiiing."

He took the paper and unfolded it carefully.

"You guys are briiiilliant," he said. "Come with meeee. Bring my heeeaaad."

They went into the kitchen, where I. Skreem made a mixture of water and ammonia and poured it on the paper. Red letters began to form.

"Whoa," said Paulie, dropping I. Skreem's head onto the floor.

Thunk.

"***Ouuuch***, you idiot. Pick it uuuuup," moaned I. Skreem. "I knew it was invisible iiiink," he said boastfully, "because I couldn't seeee iiiit!"

I. Skreem read the letter.

Thunk and ouuuch are onomatopoeia.

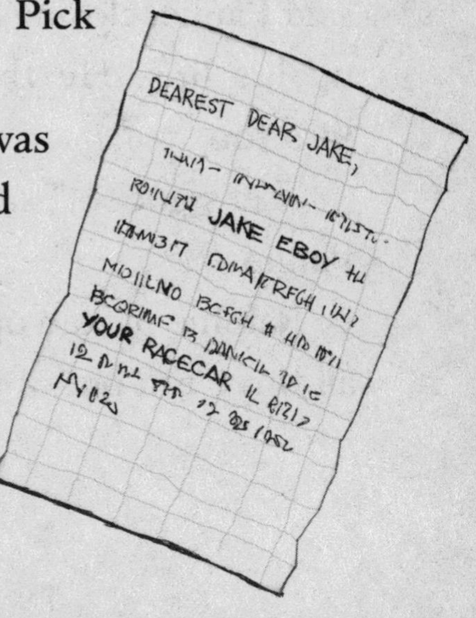

DEAREST DEAR JAKE,

JAKE EBOY

YOUR RACECAR

"Those Eboys have a son who drives a racecaaar," he said excitedly.

He got a pen and wrote on the wall:

I'M GONNA GET THAT KIIIIIIID!!!

"Hey, I know where a kid lives who drives a racecar," said Ralphie.

I. Skreem gave Ralphie a big kiss.

"Uhm, I know where that kid lives too," said Paulie, closing his eyes and puckering up his lips. He thought he deserved a kiss too.

"Let's goooo," said I. Skreem, ignoring Paulie.

Ralphie picked up I. Skreem's head and all three ran out of the house.

Mellem Bawls

At The Aunts' house, ***L'il Mellem*** was in his dad's arms bawling his eyes out.

"What's wrong?" asked Otto, rushing in.

"Dude, that little tiny aunt person sewed my baby's costume all wrong," said ***Donod***.

"***I did, did I***?" grunted FiFi. "***Haruumphff!***"

"***Wah!***" cried ***L'il Mellem***. "Bad jacket cow ***poop***!"

"Tell that melon ball kid to stand on his head and the jacket will look just fine," said FiFi. "What's the big deal?"

"I'll tell you what, ***L'il Mellem***," said Otto, taking off his own jacket, "for now you can wear this jacket. I'll go up to the attic and find you one of my old ones that'll fit you better."

Otto put his jacket on ***L'il Mellem***.

"***Sniff***," said ***L'il Mellem***, wiping his

I did, did I *and* ***poop*** *are palindromes.*
Haruumphff, ***wah***, *and* ***sniff*** *are onomatopoeia.*

eyes. “Me ***L’il Otto***,” he added proudly.

“Aw, go ***sit on a potato pan, Otis***,” said FiFi.

“My name ***L’il Otto***.” ***Mellem*** started crying all over again.

Otto glared at his aunt. ***Gnarrr!***

“You can sit in Racecar and make believe you’re driving,” Otto reassured ***Mellem***. “Would you like that?”

“***L’il Otto*** drive!” said ***L’il Mellem***, running into the garage.

“It’s okay, Aunt ***IfIf***, I know you worked hard on the costume. C’mon, I’ll give you a piggyback ride,” said Otto.

__Sit on a potato pan, Otis__ is a palindrome.
__Gnarr__ is onomatopoeia. __IfIf__ is a backward word.

"A long one?" asked FiFi.

"All the way to the attic," said Otto.

"And back," said FiFi.

"Deal," said Otto.

"Have fun," said FooFoo, "but her name isn't ***IfIf***. It's IckIck, right?" she called after them. "Or is it YukYuk?" she

mumbled to herself. "How about FooFoo? No, that's my name." She chuckled. "Unless I'm GooGoo."

The Doorbell Rang

Brrring!

Brrring is onomatopoeia.

Someone Answered It

"Who is it?" asked FooFoo.

Eeyi Eeyi Boo

FooFoo opened the door. Ralphie, Paulie, and I. Skreem stood outside in Halloween costumes.

"Boo," said Paulie.

"How adorable," said FooFoo. "What are you supposed to be?"

"I'm a bowling piglet," said Ralphie. He was holding I. Skreem's head, which was disguised as a bowling ball. ***"Snort snort."***

"Uhm, I'm this here chicken," said Paulie. ***"Gobble gobble."***

"Chickens don't say ***gobble gobble***," said Ralphie.

"How do you know? You're a piglet.

Snort and ***gobble*** *are onomatopoeia.*

***Cluck** is onomatopoeia.*

Piglets don't even speak chicken," said Paulie.

"I do. I talk to chickens all the time on the farm. All they say is ***cluck cluck***," said Ralphie.

"Well, I'm a turkey disguised as a chicken for Halloween," said Paulie.

"Oh, that's a lovely costume," said Aunt FooFoo. "One time I was an aunt disguised as an uncle and it wasn't even Halloween."

"Stooop," whined I. Skreem. His eyes darted around, trying to catch a glimpse of Otto.

"What are you supposed to be?" asked FooFoo. Except for his head, a black sheet covered his entire body.

"I'm a booowling baaaall goblin," said I. Skreem.

"How darling," said FooFoo. "Have some of these nice peanut butter, asparagus, chocolate rolls. I made them myself."

Piggy

Ralphie and Paulie grabbed about 30 pieces each.

"I'm a reaaaallly huuungry and thirsty meeean goblin. Give us a saaandwich and milk or we'll play a bad trick on you-uuu," said I. Skreem. He wanted FooFoo to leave the room so they could sneak into the house.

FooFoo was excited that someone had asked her to cook.

"How about if I make you some nice veal scaloppine and breaded lobster fingers, with a nice carrot-grapefruit milk-shake? Deelish."

"Gobble gobble," said Paulie, licking his lips.

"I'll be right back," said FooFoo. She zoomed into the kitchen.

Whoosh!

Whoosh is onomatopoeia.

The Trick

The Ice Cream Gang was left alone.

"C'mooon," whispered their leader.

They snuck into the garage. ***L'il Mellem***, wearing Otto's jacket, sat playing behind Racecar's steering wheel.

"There he is," said Paulie, who like all bad guys couldn't tell one kid from another.

"Get hiiim," orderd I. Skreem.

The three creeps grabbed ***L'il Mellem*** and ran out of the garage.

A New Name for a Bad Luck Number That Comes After 12

Otto came down from the attic with FiFi on his back and went into the garage.

"***L'il Mellem***?" called Otto. "***L'il Otto***?" he called louder.

FooFoo came back to the front door with a tray of hot food.

"Piglet?" she called. "Chicken-turkey? Bowling ball?"

Shortcut

This chapter could be about Otto and The Aunts going on a tiring and useless search for ***L'il Mellem***, but since we all know that ***L'il Mellem*** was kidnapped by the Ice Cream Gang, why don't we just tell him:

I Hear Ya!

"***Yikes!***" said Otto.

Yikes *is onomatopoeia.*

Go Go

"Change into your uncle outfits now!" said Otto, frantic. "We have to get ***Mellem*** back before I. Skreem hurts him."

The Aunts changed in a second, and they all jumped into Racecar.

Otto turned on the engine. ***Rrrrumm!***

Rrrrumm *is onomatopoeia.*

CHAPTER 15

Message Received

Click is *onomatopoeia.*

Instantly, Racecar's radio receiver began clicking out a message. ***Click, click.***

"It's a code," said Otto.

Click, click,

click, click, click, click, click, click, click, click click, click.

"It says, '***Won't we rot***,'" said Otto.

"Well, I certainly won't," said FooFoo. "Maybe BoBo over there will."

Screech is onomatopoeia.

"***Won't we rot*** is an anagram for ***Town Tower***," said Otto.

He put Racecar into gear and screeched out into the street.

Screech!

Double Dangle

Vrooom! SKID!

Racecar came to a halt in front of the Town Tower.

Music was playing, and the square was

*Vroom and **skid** are onomatopoeia.*

packed with people in costumes who had come there for the Halloween concert.

The Aunts and Otto piled out of Racecar and ran to ***Donod***, who was arranging band equipment on the outdoor stage.

"Oh dude, man, this setup is sweet. We're really gonna shred tonight," said ***Donod*** happily.

Skreeaatch is onomatopoeia.

"***Donod***, I've got some bad news," said Otto.

"No way," said ***Donod***.

"Way," said Otto. "***L'il Mellem*** was kid-napped."

"Massive bummer!" said ***Donod***, alarmed.

All of a sudden there was a horrible sound over the speakers. ***Skreeaatch!*** The music stopped, and a voice bellowed out from above them.

"I'm heeere. It's meeee. I. Skreeeeem. I know you Eboys are out theeere. I've got your son, and I'm gonna drop him off this rooooof and screeeam unless you come up heeere."

Sweat mixed with snowy skin flakes rained down onto the people below. Covered in a blanket of yucky slush, everyone stopped what they were doing and looked up. Through the downpour, they saw the Ice Cream Gang, no longer in costume, standing on the outside balcony atop the tower. Ralphie was holding up I. Skreem's head, while I. Skreem dangled ***L'il Mellem*** by the arms over the railing. Enjoying the attention, Paulie skipped around, waving at the people.

Otto instantly understood what had happened. I. Skreem had mistaken ***Mellem***, wearing the racing jacket, for Otto. He didn't know how those boobs Ralphie and Paulie had gotten out of jail, or why I. Skreem had mentioned his parents, but right now he didn't care. All he could think about was saving ***L'il Mellem***, who was in grave danger. And it was all his fault.

A Familiar Pumpkin

"I'm not kiddiiing. I'm gonna screeeam in a minuuute," whined I. Skreem.

Everyone in the crowd ran. The only ones not moving were Otto, FiFi, FooFoo, ***Donod***, a person dressed as a pumpkin, and another person dressed as a roasted marshmallow.

__Psssst__ is onomatopoeia.

"Ugly monster scary doo doo!" wailed ***L'il Mellem***.

"Psssst," Otto whispered to ***Donod*** and The Aunts. "Distract him."

"How, dude?" asked ***Donod***.

"Keep him talking. ***IrfIrf***, ***OrfOrf***, put your pimple receivers on. I'm going up." Otto turned on his freckle transmitter.

"No, it's too dangerous," said FooFoo, stamping her foot again. ***Clump.***

FiFi fell to the ground and held on to Otto's leg. She was hysterical. "Don't go. It's all my fault. I'll go. I hope there's an elevator," she sobbed.

"Good idea, Irv," said FooFoo. "You go."

Otto wiggled

free of FiFi and raced off.

As the roasted-marshmallow person brushed past The Aunts, a man's voice whispered, "It's all right. We'll look after him."

"Who was that marshmallow?" asked FooFoo.

"I don't know," said FiFi, "but I feel like I've seen that pumpkin before."

Not Bernard

Otto snuck over to the back of the tower. The pumpkin and the marshmallow followed.

"I'm dropping hiiim," said I. Skreem, squeezing ***L'il Mellem***.

"Ouch, oooch, achhh, yuk yuk," said ***L'il Mellem***.

"Chill out, dude, don't hurt my tiny son," yelled ***Donod***.

"He's nooot your son," yelled I. Skreem.

"Is too," yelled ***Donod***.

"Is nooot," yelled I. Skreem.

"He looks like your son," said FooFoo, "but he also looks a little bit like that nephew of mine, what's his name?"

"Bernard," said FiFi, rolling her eyes.

*Ouch, oooch, achhh, and **yuk** are onomatopoeia.*

"Ask him if his name is Bernard," yelled FooFoo, still trying to distract I. Skreem.

"It's noooot Bernaaard," said I. Skreem.

"Just ask him, dude," yelled ***Donod***.

"All right already," yelled Ralphie. "Is your name Bernard?"

"Me no barnyard," said ***L'il Mellem***, and he popped Ralphie in the face. Ralphie dropped I. Skreem's head. ***Thunk!***

"Hey, my middle name is Bernard," yelled Paulie to ***Donod***. "Maybe you're my daddy."

"Pick up my heeead," whined I. Skreem.

Engine #8

Otto ejected his shoe computer and pressed *Option 23*. Racecar morphed into a Fire Truck–Car. With the remote, Otto moved the fire car to the back of the tower and whispered, "**Put it up**," which was a **voice command** for the **fire ladder**.

***Put it up** is a palindrome.*

Just as Otto set his foot on the first rung, the pumpkin and the marshmallow surrounded him.

"What do you want?" asked Otto suspiciously. He was about to tap his freckle transmitter.

"It's us, Jake." The pumpkin had a woman's voice.

"Yes, Son, it's Mom and Dad," said the marshmallow.

Otto almost fainted.

CHAPTER 20

Reunion

But he didn't.

He hugged his marshmallow dad, who was very squishy, and he tried to hug his pumpkin mom, but her pumpkin shell was kind of hard.

"We don't have much time. We'd better get up to the tower and save that little boy," she said.

"Right," said Otto's dad. "I brought the scream deflector. Make sure you stay behind it." They started quickly up the ladder.

"Okay," said Otto. Even though he couldn't see their faces, the excitement of being reunited with his parents made his head spin. He thought he was dreaming.

"Yeoow!" yelled ***L'il Mellem***, and he blew a loud raspberry. ***Pzzzzzt!*** That brought Otto back to reality.

"What about ***L'il Mellem***?" asked Otto. "He won't be behind the deflector."

"That's true," agreed the marshmallow. "It's not a perfect plan."

"We are going to give ourselves up in exchange for the toddler," said Otto's mom sadly.

Otto felt like he'd been slapped in the

Yeoow and pzzzzzt are onomatopoeia.

Whack is onomatopoeia.

face. ***Whack!*** "No," he said, "I can't lose you again."

"I'm afraid we have no choice," said the marshmallow.

"I need an idea," said Otto. "If someone only had a lightbulb."

The pumpkin put her hand inside her shell and lit up like a jack-o-lantern.

The results were instantaneous.

"I need a digital copy of I. Skreem's scream," said Otto, "so I can download it into my shoe computer and analyze it. If I know what it's made of, I might be able to think of a way to neutralize it."

"We have one, Jakey boy," said the marshmallow. "It's in my elbow computer."

"Turn it on, please," said Otto, kicking off his left shoe and catching it in his hand. He pressed his universal remote downloader, which was at the end of his shoelace, and pointed it at his father's elbow. ***Shlikk!***

"We have to keep moving," said Otto's mom. His parents were out of breath from the steep climb.

Shlikk *is onomatopoeia.*

Huff! Huff!

"You keep going. I'll catch up," said Otto, who moved much faster than they did. "This will only take a couple of seconds." Otto sat down on a rung of the ladder. His eyes scanned the data moving through his shoe. ***Shlattch shlaaak shlizzzl!***

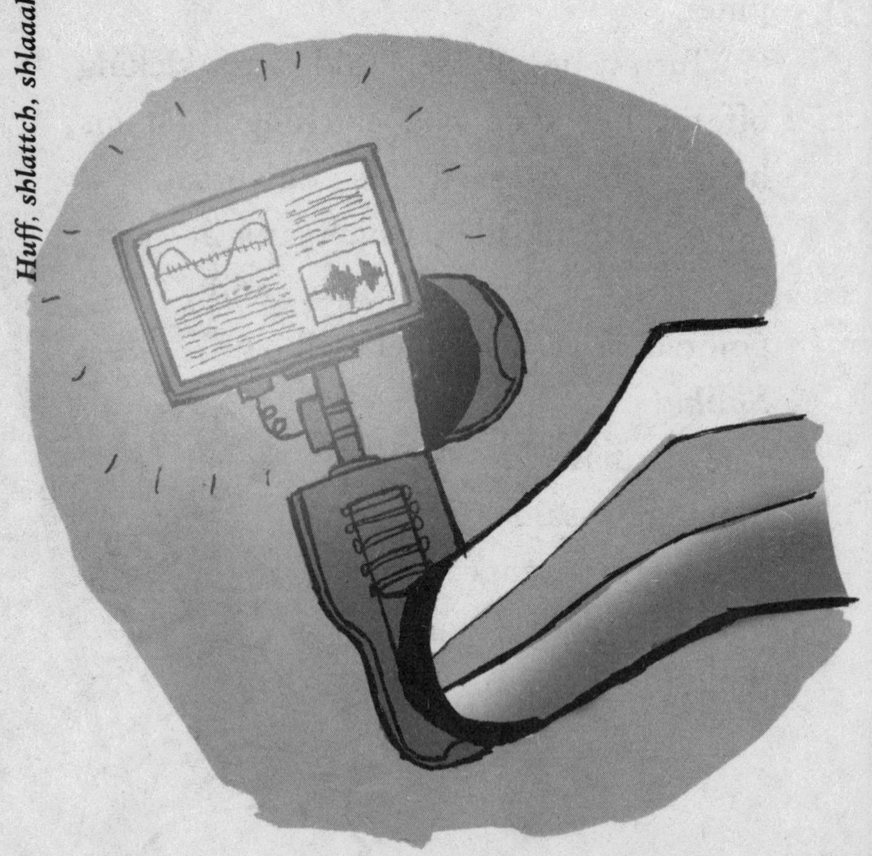

*Huff, **shlattch**, **shlaaak**, and **shlizzzl** are onomatopoeia.*

A Foot Thought

"If I don't hear from those Eboys in one minuuute, I'm screeeaming and drop-piiing," yelled I. Skreem.

"***Pssst***, Paulie," whispered Ralphie. "C'mere."

"What's up?" asked Paulie.

"Stop talking behind my baaaack," said I. Skreem.

Ralphie whispered, "I was just thinking this thought."

"You mean, like in your brain?" asked Paulie, impressed.

"Where else, you bean head," said Ralphie.

"In your stomach, your back, your foot, or your butt, you ignoramus," said Paulie.

"Oh, maybe not your butt. Your butt probably still hurts too much to think," said Paulie.

"Whatever," said Ralphie. "The thing is, see, if this guy screams, see, we're gonna get hit, see, because we're standing right next to him and holding his head and all, see?"

"***Uhh***, that sounds like a foot thought because it has the word 'standing' in it," said Paulie.

"Yeah sure, a foot thought," said Ralphie. "So why don't you hold this here head, and I'll go get us some help."

"If I hold this here head now, you have to hold it three times tomorrow because you owe me two holds." Paulie looked at the pad he used to kept track.

"Sure," said Ralphie. "Just take the head."

"Who are you gonna get to help us?" asked Paulie.

Uhh is onomatopoeia.

"Batman," said Ralphie sarcastically.

"What if he's not in his Bat Cave?" asked Paulie.

"Then I'll get Ma," said Ralphie.

"Tell her to bring the ham," said Paulie happily.

Bwoing!

Otto's shoe computer went berserk, racing through millions of combinations of binary numbers to find the essence of I.Skreem's scream. ***Sktzakktchitchkknnnrr!***

"C'mon," called Otto's dad, "we're almost at the top."

This wasn't good. Otto was worried. He spoke into his freckle transmitter.

"***IrfIrf***, ***OrfOrf***, go to Racecar and await orders."

"On the job!" said FiFi, as FooFoo picked her up and ran with ***Donod*** to the fire car.

Then the unthinkable happened.

Bwoing *and* ***sktzakktchitchkknnnrr*** *are onomatopoeia.*

Bwoing! Whap! Twang! The calculation was too much for the tiny computer. It broke into a zillion pieces.

*"**Arggh!**"* exclaimed Otto, looking down at the mess in his hands.

"Wait! I've got an idea!" he said.

He ran up the ladder to his mom and dad.

"What did you say your singing notes were?" he asked.

"Dad's is an E and mine is a C," said the pumpkin.

"Okay," said Otto, "I don't know if this is going to work, but it's the only chance we've got. When I give the signal, sing your notes as loud as you can."

"What song should we sing?" asked the marshmallow.

"How about Doctor Demento's 'We're Coming to Take You Away, ***Ha-Haaa***'?" said Otto.

Just then the tower door opened.

Whap, twang, arggh, *and **ha-haaa** are onomatopoeia.*

Flying Goons

Ralphie came running out, gobs of sweat oozing from his pores onto the ground. Slipping on his own gunk, he slid across the balcony and plunged headfirst over the ladder. ***Oof flip splat!***

Oof flip splat is onomatopoeia.

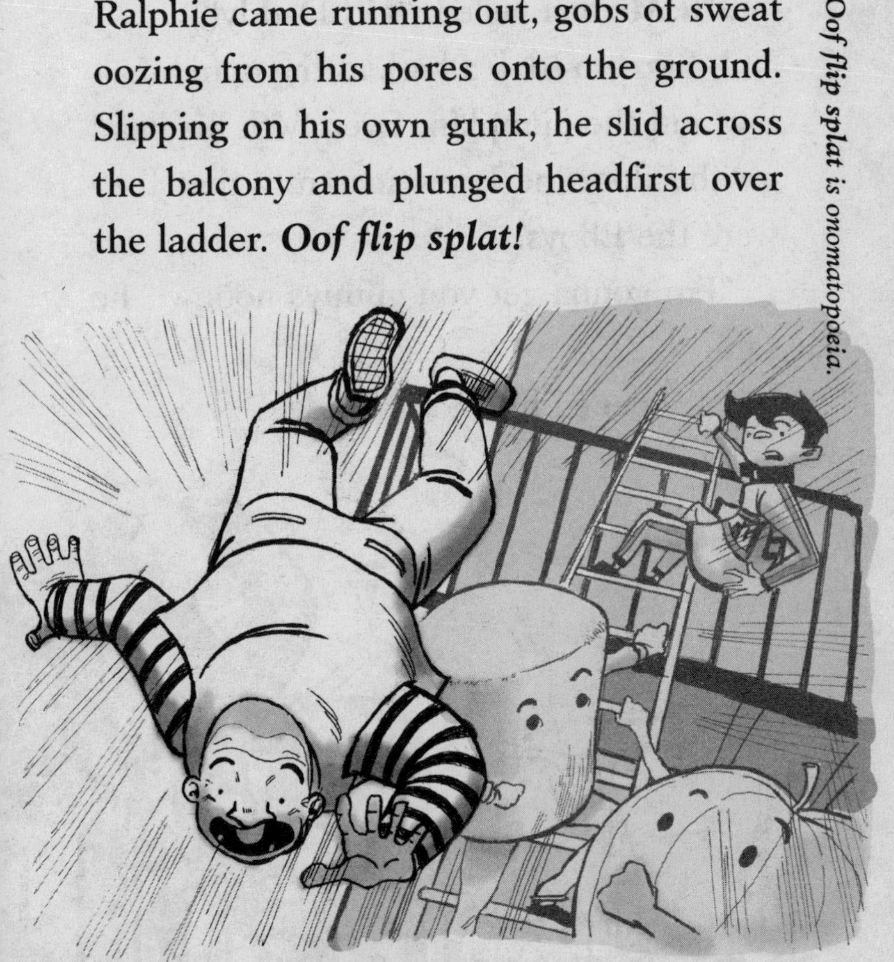

Splam is *onomatopoeia.*

Paulie took one look at Otto and thought he was ***L'il Mellem***'s ghost. Scared out of his mind, he dropped I. Skreem's head and jumped off the balcony. ***Splam!***

L'il Mellem yelled, "***L'il*** Daddy!"

I. Skreem took a look at the marshmallow and the pumpkin. Even with his head on the floor, he knew instantly that they were the Eboys.

"I'm gonna get you guuuys nooow!" he said.

He opened his mouth wide. . . .

The Signal

"*SING!*" said Otto.

CHAPTER 25

Eeeeeeeeeyiiiiiiiiiiiiiiyeeeeeeeeee!!!!!!!!

I. Skreem let out the loudest, shrillest, longest scream he had ever screamed in his whole screaming life.

At precisely the same time, Eleanor, Hogarth, and Otto sang in the notes C, E, and G:

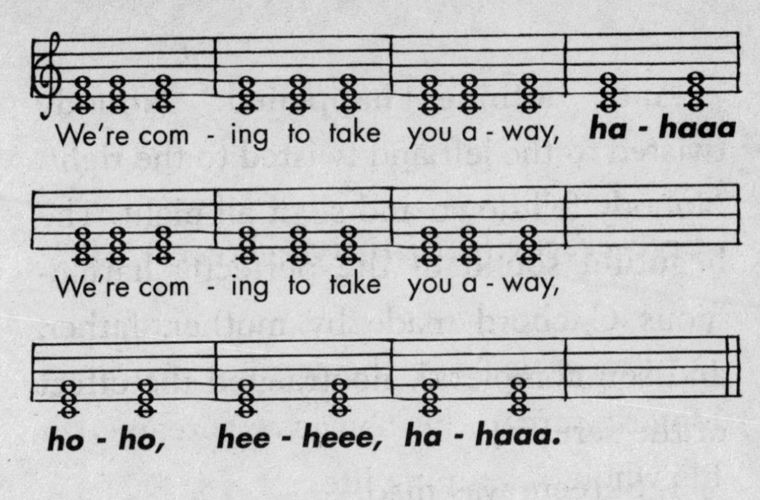

Zap! Zap! Zip! Electricity filled the air as screams collided.

And nothing happened. Nobody twisted to the left and twisted to the right. Nobody fell down and slept all night. The beautiful sound of the perfectly harmonious C chord made by mother, father, and son completely neutralized the effect of the scream.

I. Skreem was mad.

"***Mellem*** sing," said ***L'il Mellem***.

Whoops

I. Skreem dropped ***L'il Mellem*** off the tower.

"***Mellem*** fall," said ***L'il Mellem***.

Last Chance

Otto never got to put the finishing touches on Racecar's surprise disguise, but he knew it was his only hope for saving ***L'il Mellem***. He crossed his fingers, arms, toes, legs, and elbows.

Otto yelled into his freckle transmitter, *"Option 338, Heli-Car!"*

Wipeout

FiFi was behind the wheel of the Fire Truck–Car. She got the message on her pimple and pressed *338* into the dashboard option grid.

Meanwhile, the wind tossing him around, ***L'il Mellem*** tumbled down the side of the tower.

"My little dude is going to totally wipe out," cried ***Donod***. "What a mighty bummer!"

"Hold on to your butts," said FiFi. "We're morphing!"

Shaking, Racecar sounded like he was going to explode. ***Pow, pop, pop, pop, kzakk!*** But Racecar did not change into anything.

Pow, pop, and kzakk are onomatopoeia.

Amazingly, a split second later, the three passengers felt themselves rapidly rising as the Fire Truck–Car lifted off the ground. They looked up to see the ladder transformed into an **overhead propeller**.

Racecar had become a

Fire-Copter.

Whirr

Whirr is onomatopoeia.

Otto couldn't believe what he saw. He must have crossed some wires in his Heli-Car design, but a Fire-Copter would work just fine. What a lucky break.

"Watch I. Skreem while I steer," he yelled to his parents.

Using his pocket watch remote, Otto steered the Fire-Copter under ***L'il Mellem***.

His mission was to get his friend to fall directly into the empty hole in the center of the propeller's four blades.

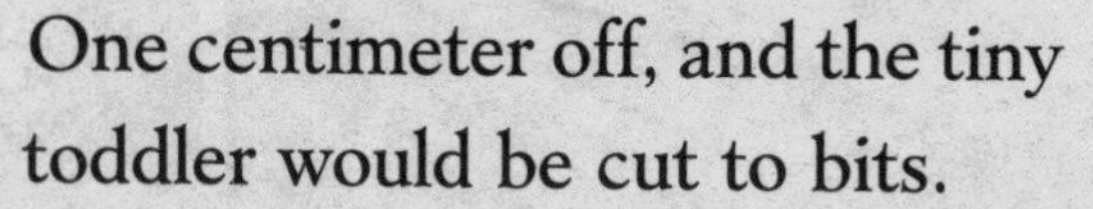

One centimeter off, and the tiny toddler would be cut to bits.

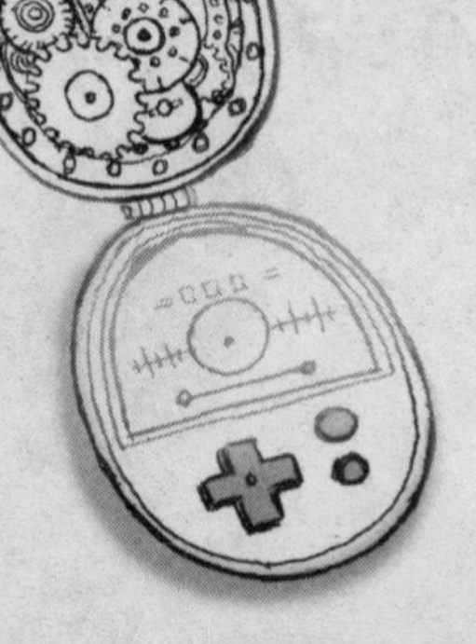

Swish

Luckily, as the world's greatest racecar driver, Otto never doubted his skill. Steering was his specialty.

He was also great at math, doing dozens of problems every day to keep in shape. He held up his *Wind Meter*, which was in his ring, and instantly calculated the rest of ***Mellem***'s fall.

Now ***Mellem*** was coming down fast.

Swish *is onomatopoeia.*

Otto steered the Fire-Copter to the final coordinates and pressed 'hover.'

"Prepare for toddler!" he spoke into his transmitter.

FiFi held the wheel steady.

FooFoo and ***Donod*** put out their hands.

Mellem twirled down directly through the center hole of the propeller and fell gracefully into his father's arms. ***Swish!***

"Most excellent, little dude," said ***Donod***.

"***Mellem*** drive," said ***L'il Mellem***.

The Old Days Remembered

"Let's get out of here," said Otto to his folks.

"One second, my little genius," said the marshmallow.

I. Skreem's scream wasn't working very well now. He had overdone it and was getting laryngitis.

Otto's dad handcuffed I. Skreem to a post, while his mom squirted Freeze down his throat and called the police.

"Sorry, old friend," said Mr. Eboy, "you could have been the best crime fighter in history."

"You still can be," said Mrs. Eboy. "It's never too late to turn your life around."

"Keep dreamiiing, you lamo bozos,"

croaked I. Skreem. “I’m still gonna get you guuuys!”

The Fire-Copter was hovering ***level*** with the balcony now.

Whip whip! FiFi opened the door, allowing an entry plank to unfold.

The Eboys walked into the Fire-Copter, and they all took off.

Level *is a palindrome.* ***Whip*** *is onomatopoeia.*

Together

"I'll take over the wheel," said Otto.

"No," said Otto's mom. "I can't wait any longer to hug my little boy. FiFi, please keep flying."

"Your name is FiFi?" said FooFoo. "That's just ridiculous."

The Eboys got into the very backseat with their son and took off their costumes. Otto looked at his parents for the first time since he was two. He couldn't help it. He was so happy, he started to cry.

They hugged and kissed each other. There was no need for words.

"Who are those people?" FooFoo asked FiFi.

"They're your sister and brother-in-law.

Jake's parents," explained FiFi. She was kind of teary as well. But only because she had dropped a sewing needle down her underpants and it was sticking into her left butt cheek.

A Turn of Events

Just then Otto noticed a small airplane closing in on them. ***Roar.***

"What is that guy doing?" said Otto. "It's dangerous for airplanes to get too close.

"Rats, ***Ele***!" said Otto's dad to his wife.

"What is it, ***Hogob***?" she asked.

"I'm getting a message in my eyelid receptor," he said. "Rats and purple pus! What terrible timing."

****Roar*** is onomatopoeia. **Ele** and **Hogob** are palindromes.*

Pip is a palindrome.

"What does it say?" asked Otto.

"This is very bad news. We must be going. Somebody needs our help desperately," said Hogarth.

"Oh no," said Otto's mom.

"Yes," said Hogarth. "There's our ride."

The small plane pulled alongside the Fire-Copter. It had a British flag painted on the tail. Otto recognized the driver.

"Mr. ***Rabbar***," he said, surprised.

"***Pip pip***, lad. Jolly good vehicle you have there," said ***Rabbar***. "Smashing."

The roof of the airplane opened up.

"Please, ***Hogoh***, just let me give Otto eleven more kisses," said his mom, not wanting to let go of him.

"Twelve," said his dad, not wanting to leave either.

"How about blankteen?" begged Otto.

Otto's mom and dad kissed their son blankteen times plus one more for good luck. Then they ejected themselves out of the hole in the center of the Fire-Copter's propeller blades and in through the open roof of the plane.

"We'll be back as soon as we possibly can," said Otto's mom.

"But why can't someone else go? Who needs your help?" asked Otto.

"Your sister," called Otto's dad as their airplane veered off and disappeared into the clouds.

Waaaay

“MY SISTER???????????????????”
said Otto.

“Aunt ***IfIf***, Aunt **OofOof**, did you know I had a sister?” he asked.

The Aunts answered at the same time:

“Yes,” said FooFoo. “No,” said FiFi.

“I mean no,” said FooFoo. “I mean yes,” said FiFi.

“No way, dude!” said ***Donod***. “You’ve got a dudette!”

“No way,” said Otto.

“Way, nik nik,” said ***L’il Mellem***.

The Pits

Otto had a zillion different emotions running through him. It was just too much to handle. There was only one thing to do at a time like this:

sing!

But the concert at Town Tower had been called off because of a crime scene investigation. Also because Ralphie's fall from the ladder had ended with him smashing through the concrete and creating yet another hole in the earth. His sweat had mixed with the underground dirt and created a huge bottomless mud pit. Lucky for Paulie, he too had landed in the mud after jumping off the balcony.

Squish!

Squish is *onomatopoeia.*

Ralphie, big and fat, was having a hard time keeping his head above the mud. He clung to Paulie, who paddled around as best he could.

"I hope Batman gets here soon," gurgled Paulie.

Small Bugs

Considering the events of the day, Otto insisted on changing the name of the band from the Screaming Oranges to the ***Bed Lice*** Deflectors. ***Donod*** called the rest of their band, a guy named Larry, who played a really lousy trumpet. He told him that the concert was moved to The Aunts' house.

***Bed lice** is an anagram for **decibel** (which is a measurement of sound).*

Otto landed the Fire-Copter in a dark field and transformed it back into Racecar.

They arrived at the garage a few minutes later. Otto pressed the remote, and the garage door rolled open.

Piles and piles of Raisinets cascaded through the opening. The entire garage was filled with them. Otto and the others were almost crushed in the avalanche.

Dood is a palindrome.

Otto didn't have to wonder how they got there. He knew. "My mom and dad got these for me," he said proudly.

"Sweeeet!" said ***Donod***.

"Far out, ***dood***," said ***L'il Mellem***.

Chocolate

The band never played better. That's because they always played awful.

FiFi tap-danced atop boxes of Raisinets until her shoes got too full of melted chocolate and squashed raisins, and she got stuck to the floor.

Mellem took breaks from eating Raisinets to go trick-or-treating to everyone at the party. They all gave him Raisinets.

FooFoo served up massive amounts of veal shanks and ***Feeble Tom's Motel Beef*** à la mode. Larry ate most of it.

Otto was very proud of the song he wrote. He put on his antenna hat, hoping that his mom and dad and sister could tune it in.

Not a Banana Baton

by Otto

(In the note of G

Background by everyone else

in any note they want)

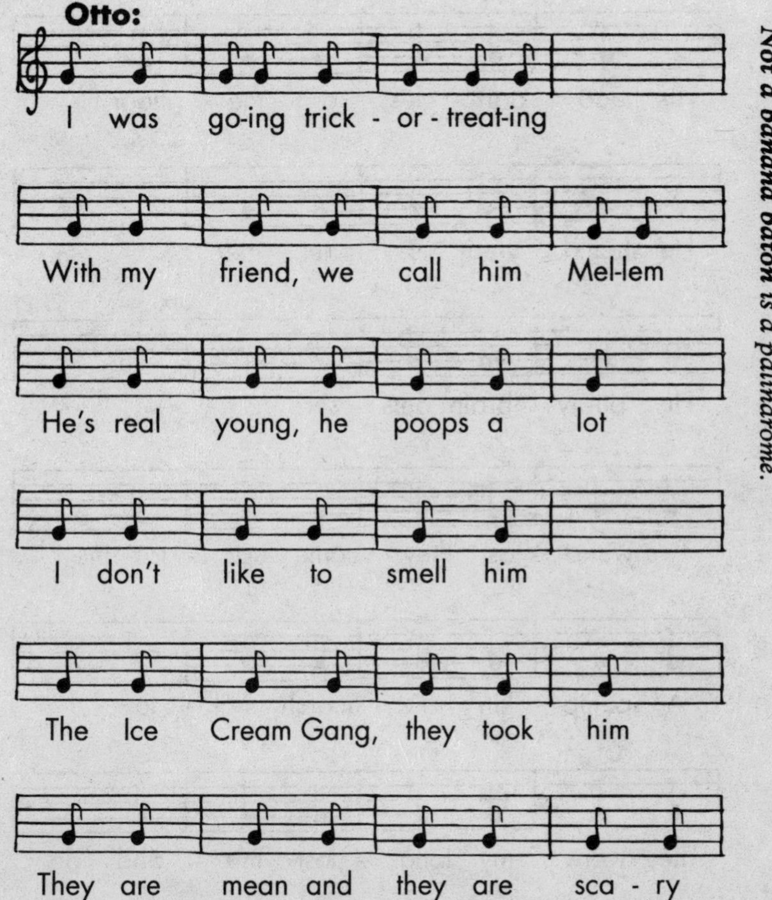

Not a banana baton is a palindrome.

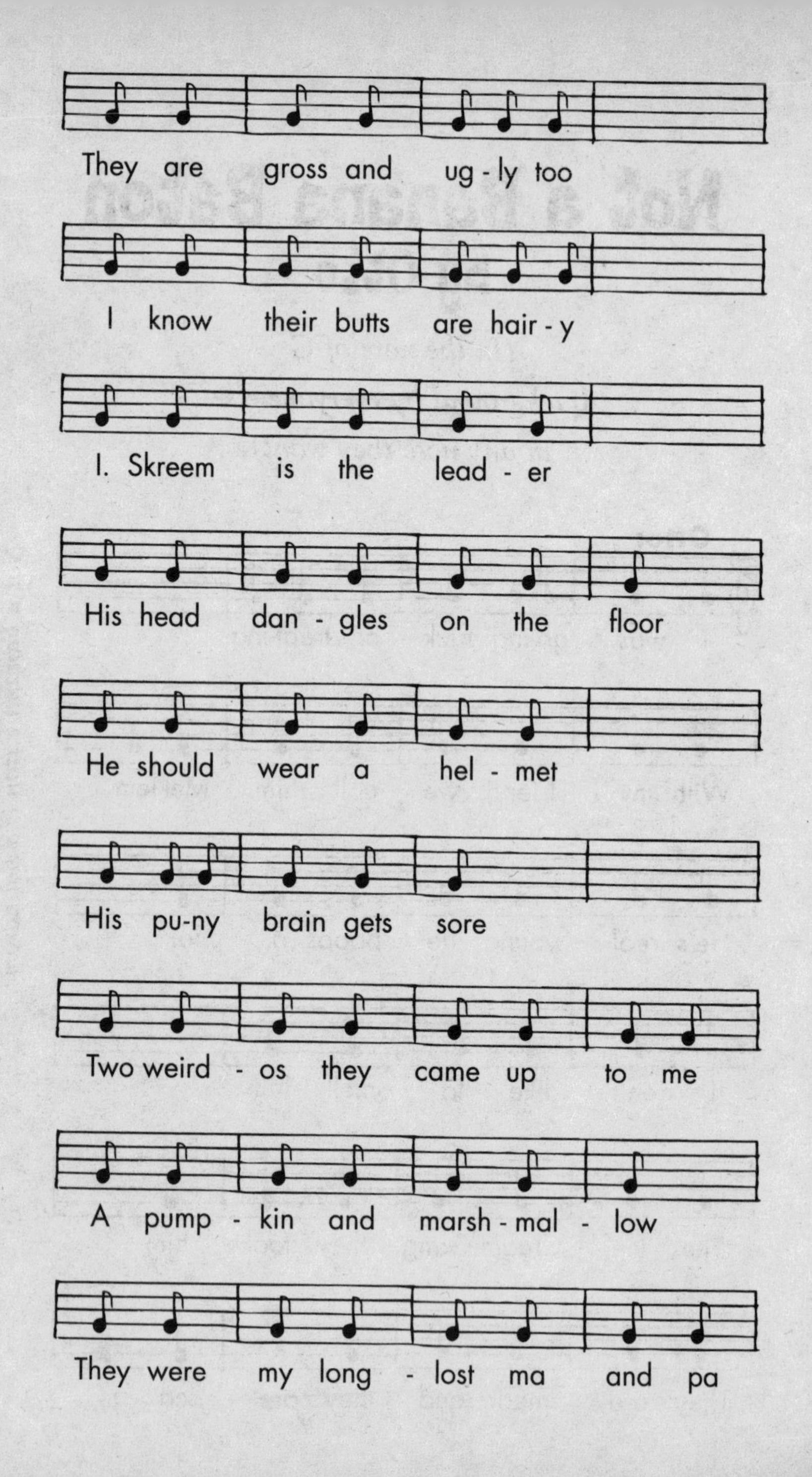
They are gross and ug - ly too
I know their butts are hair - y
I. Skreem is the lead - er
His head dan - gles on the floor
He should wear a hel - met
His pu-ny brain gets sore
Two weird - os they came up to me
A pump - kin and marsh - mal - low
They were my long - lost ma and pa

I thought that they were swell - o
When we got to - ge - ther
We pro - duced some notes
That sound - ed sweet and shat - tered screams
And was dan - ger - ous to goats
The great - est thing of all is
I found out I have a sis - ter
I won - der what her note is
And why my big toe has a blis - ter

Then Otto ate Raisinets until his stomach burst.

Then he fell asleep. On Racecar. With ***L'il Mellem***. And ***Donod***. And The Aunts. And Larry.